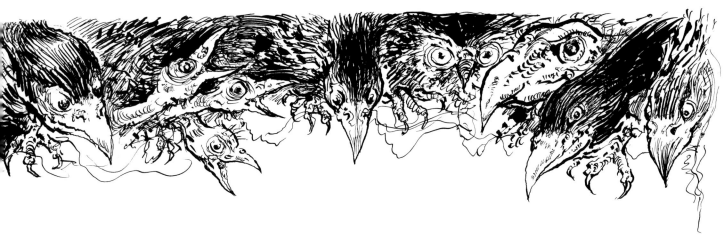

BYE, BYE BIRDIE

To Eric Drib

BYE, BYE BIRDIE

Shirley Hughes

JONATHAN CAPE
LONDON

Published by Jonathan Cape 2009

2 4 6 8 10 9 7 5 3 1

First published in Great Britain in 2009 by
Jonathan Cape
Random House, 20 Vauxhall Bridge Road,
London SW1V 2SA

www.rbooks.co.uk

Addresses for companies within The Random House Group Limited can be found at:
www.randomhouse.co.uk/offices.htm

The Random House Group Limited Reg. No. 954009

A CIP catalogue record for this book is available from the British Library

ISBN 9780224080750

The Random House Group Limited supports The Forest Stewardship Council (FSC),
the leading international forest certification organisation. All our titles that are printed on Greenpeace approved FSC certified
paper carry the FSC logo.Our paper procurement policy can be found at www.rbooks.co.uk/environment

Printed and bound in China by C&C Offset Printing Co., Ltd

Bye, Bye Birdie

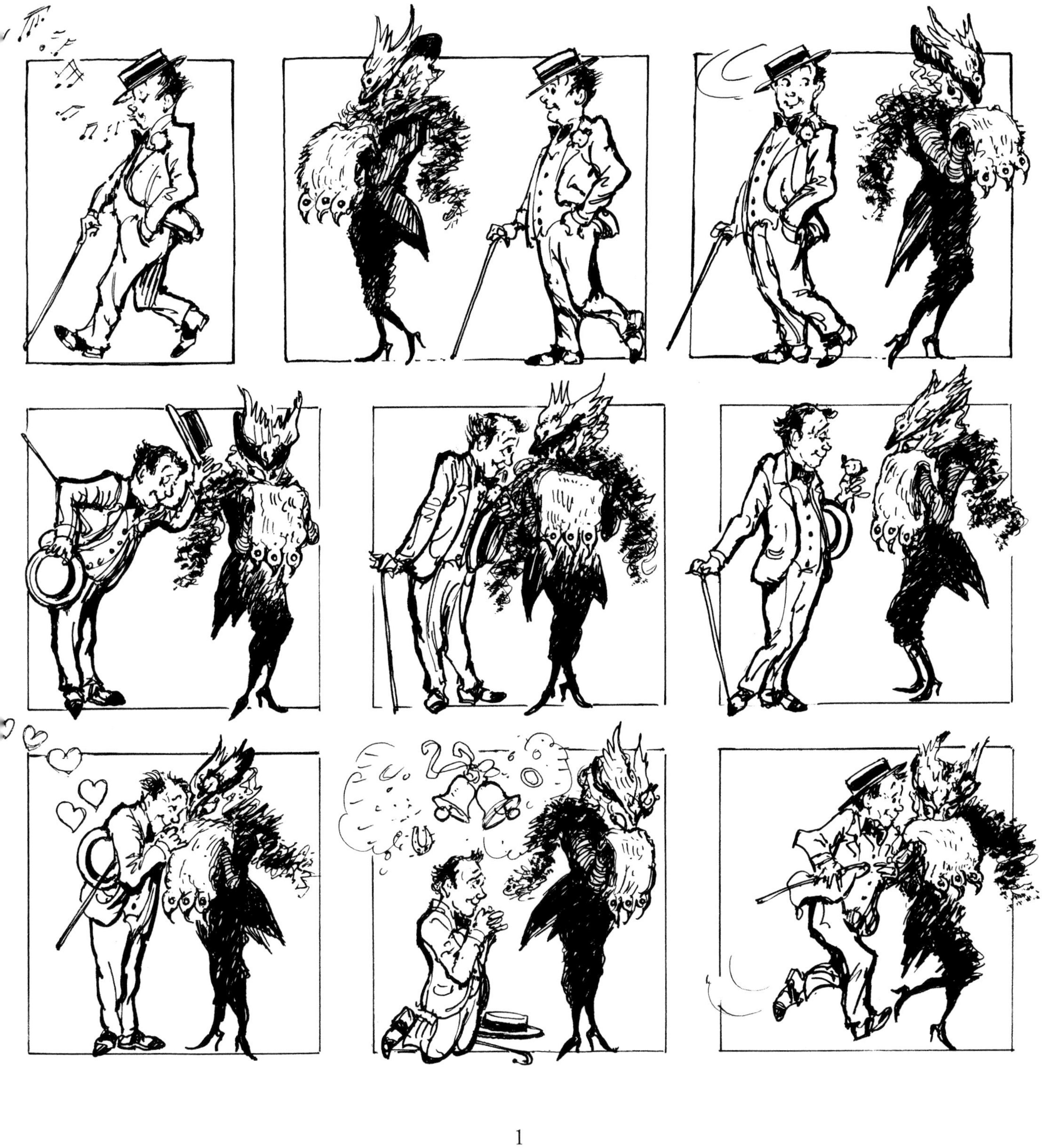

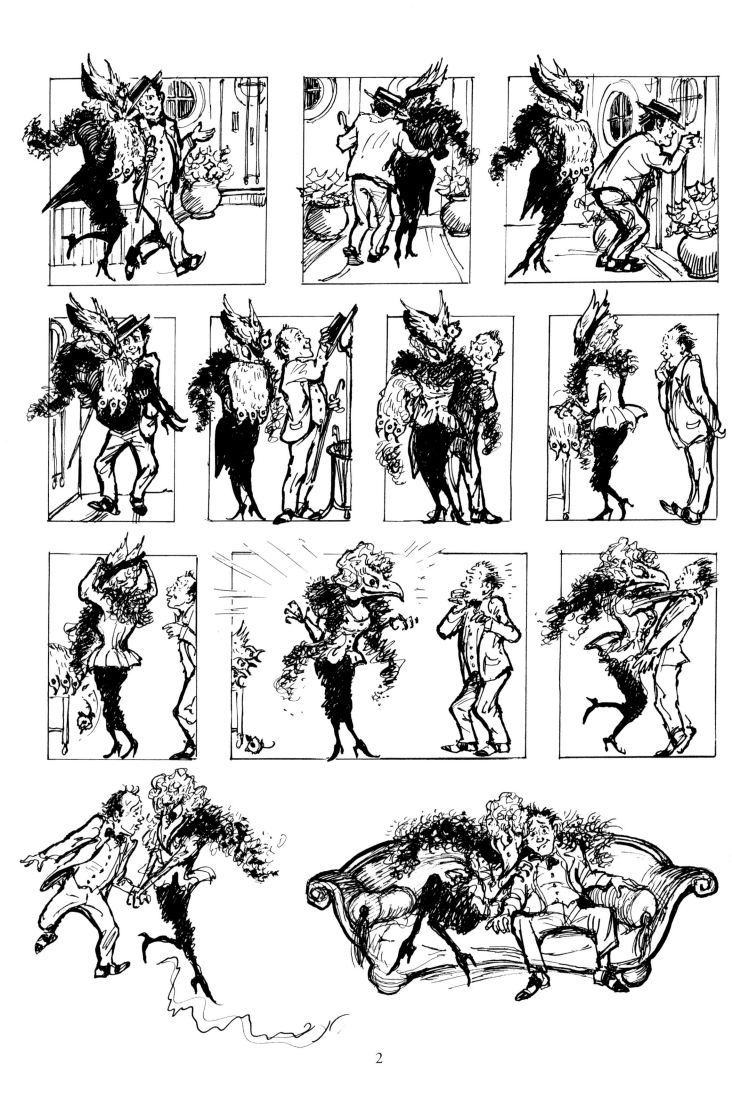

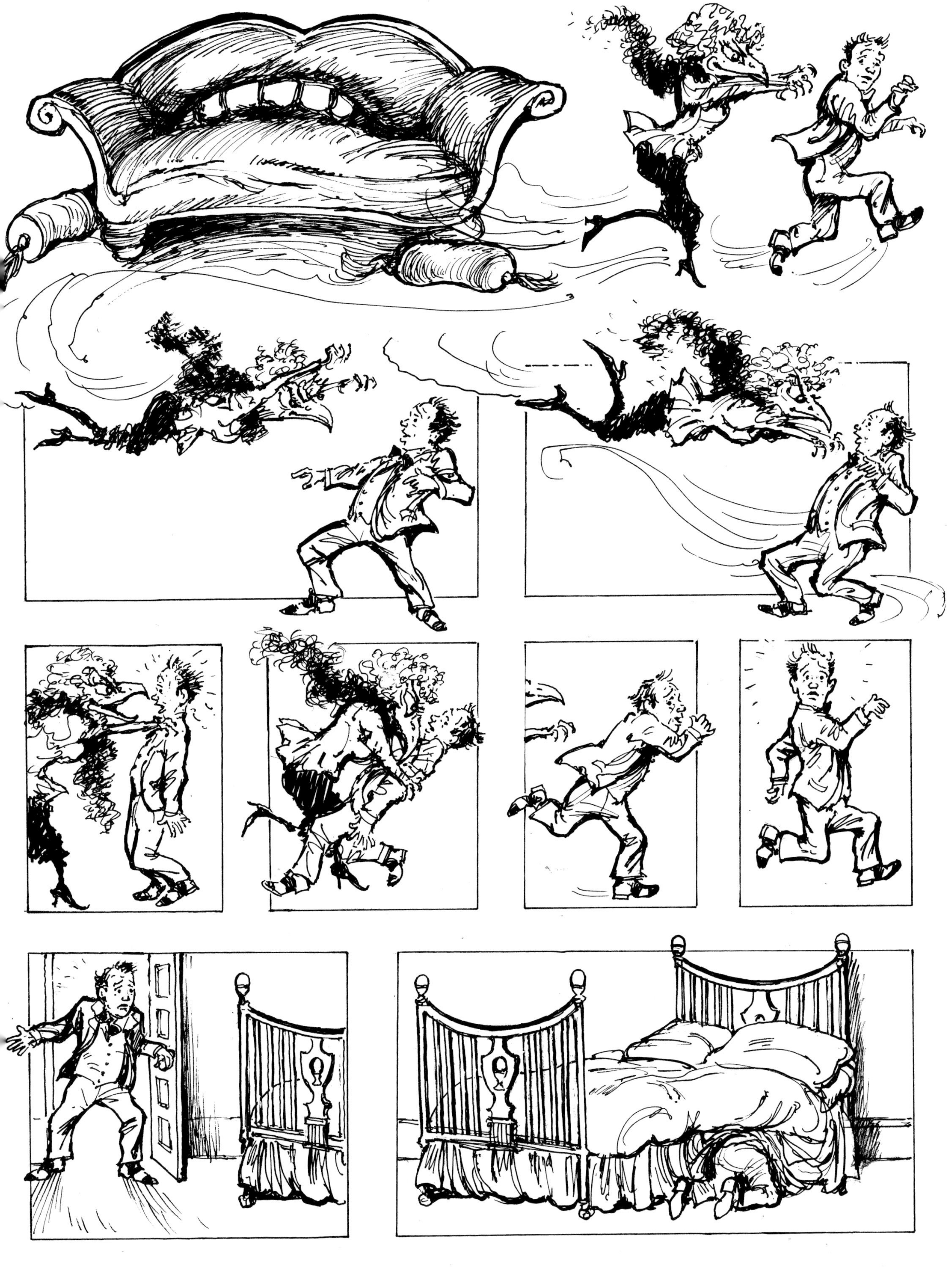

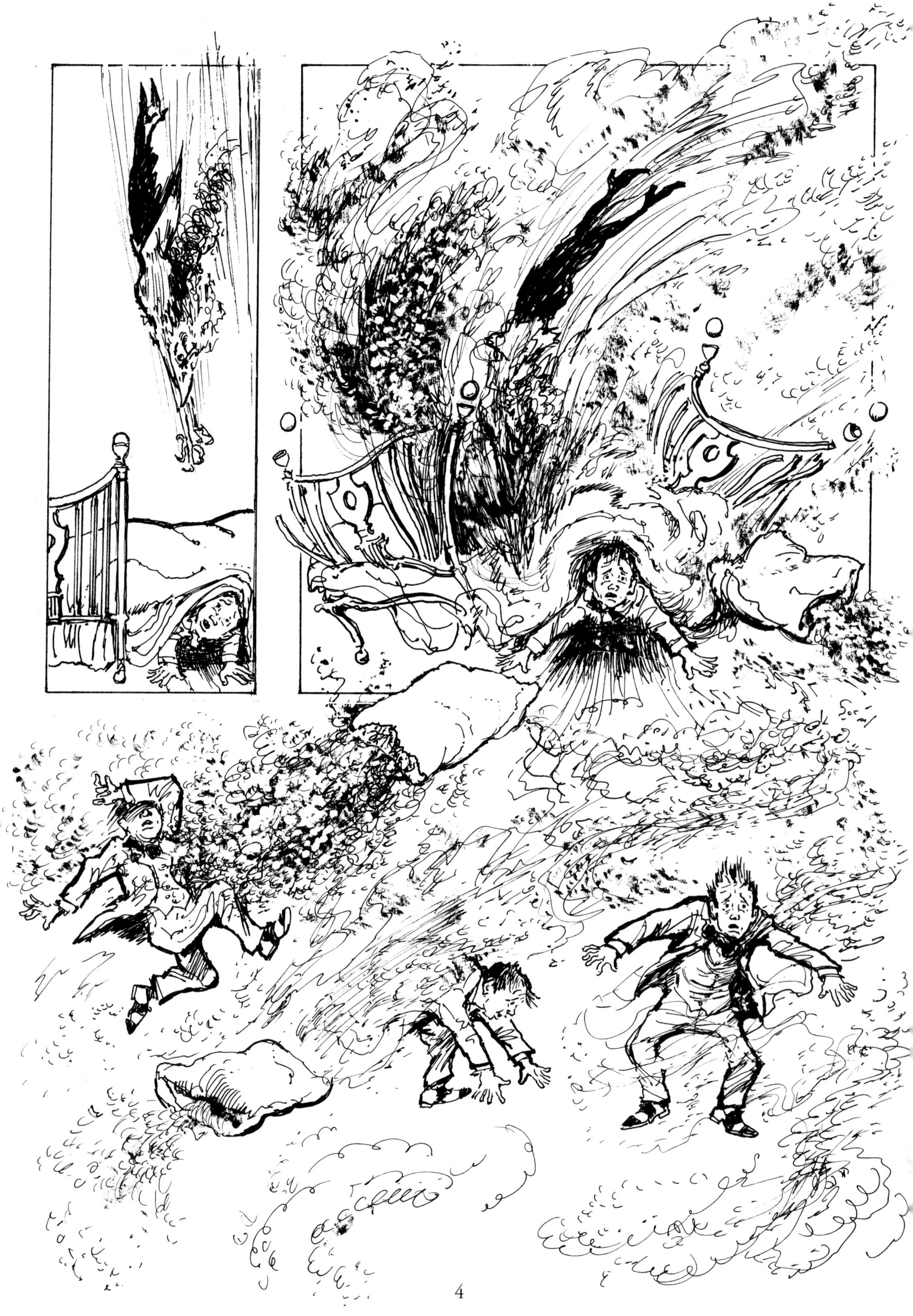

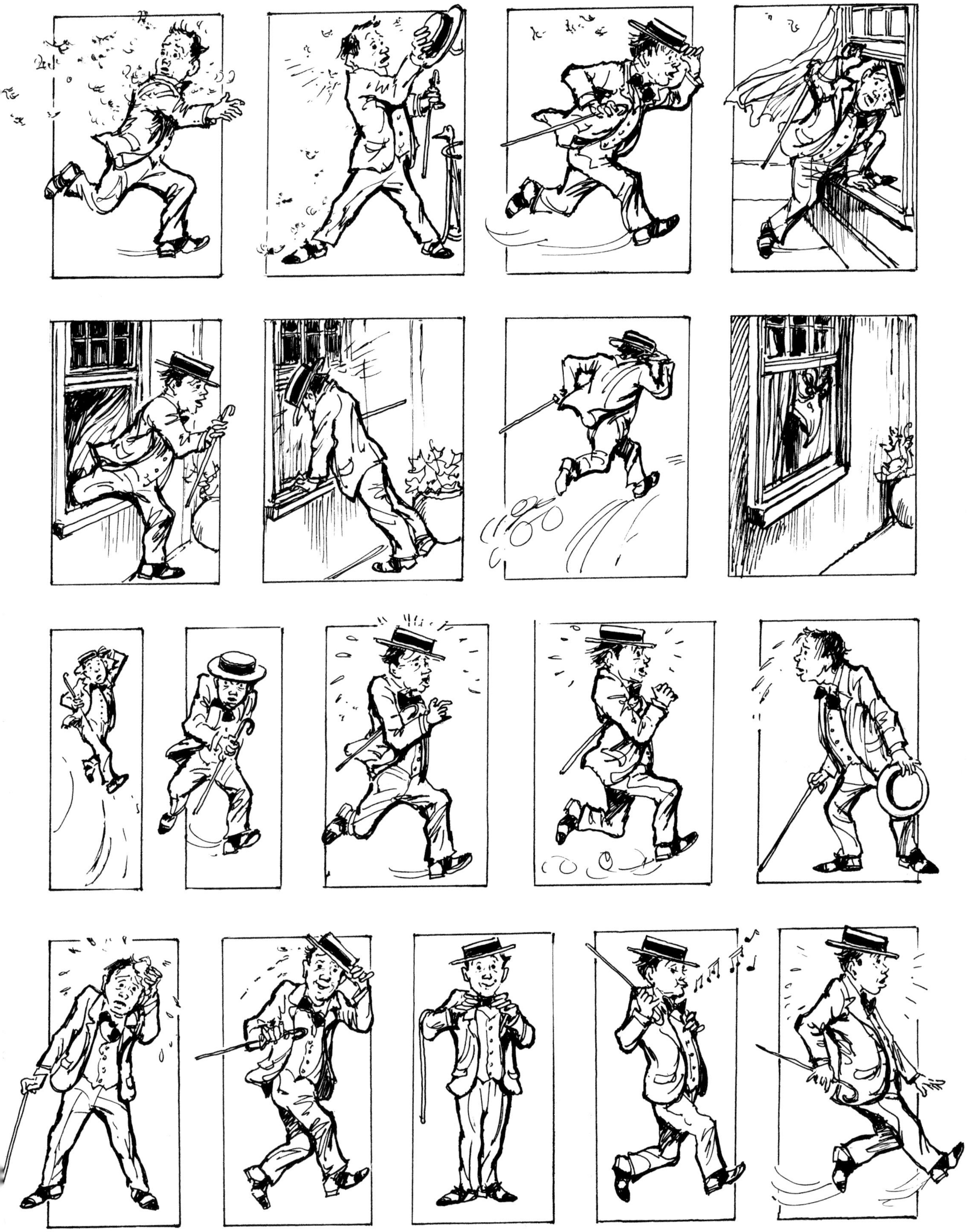

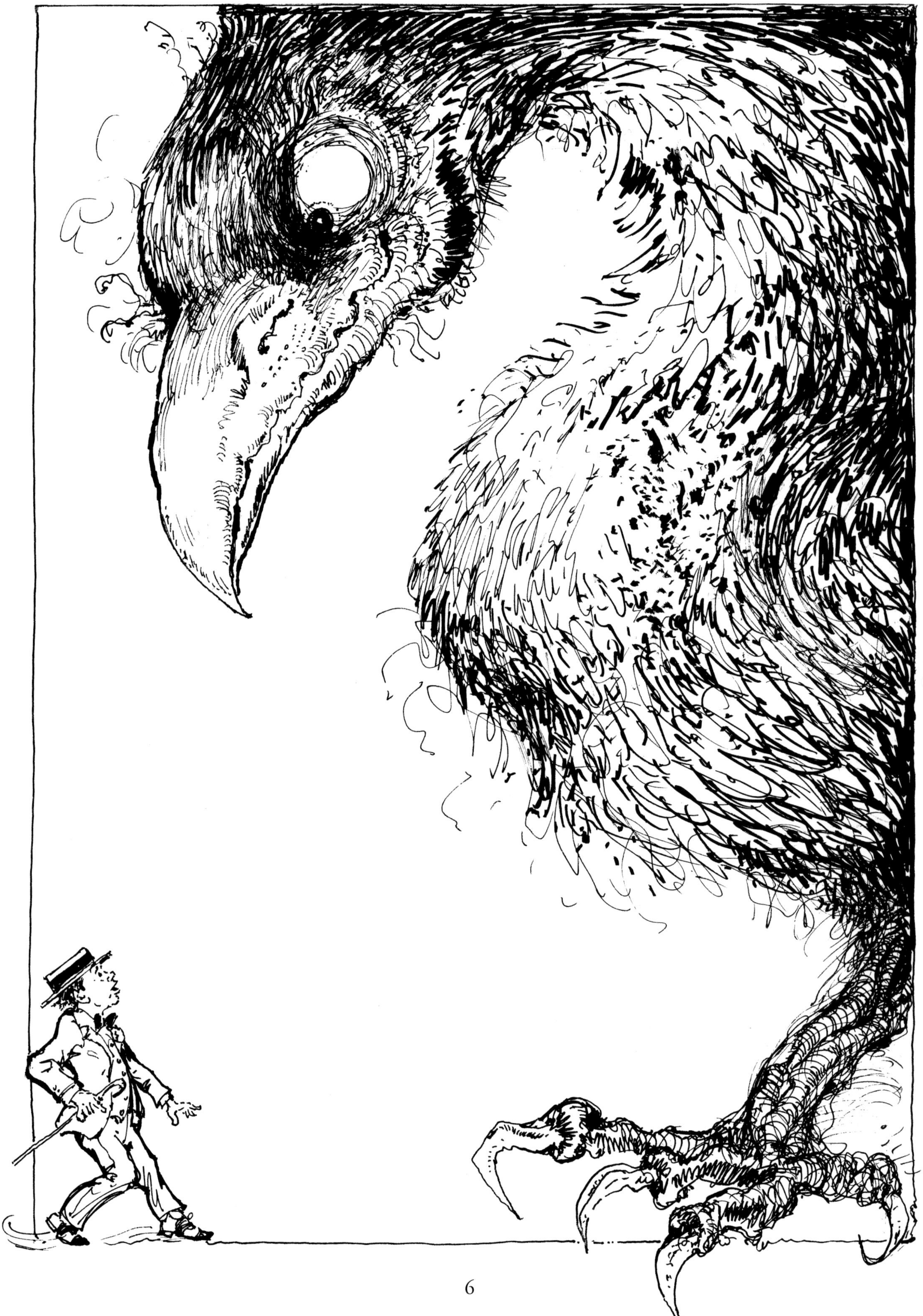

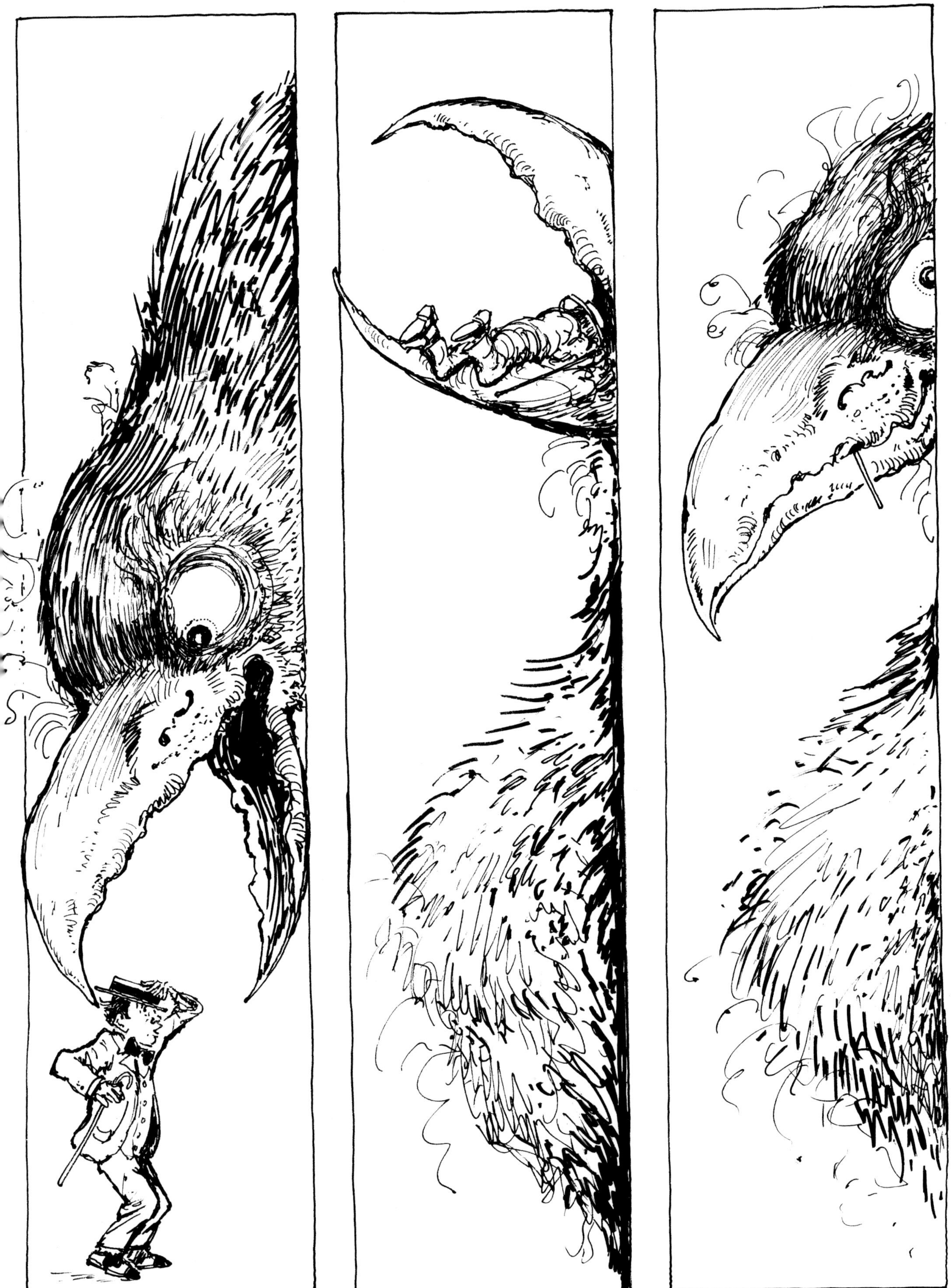

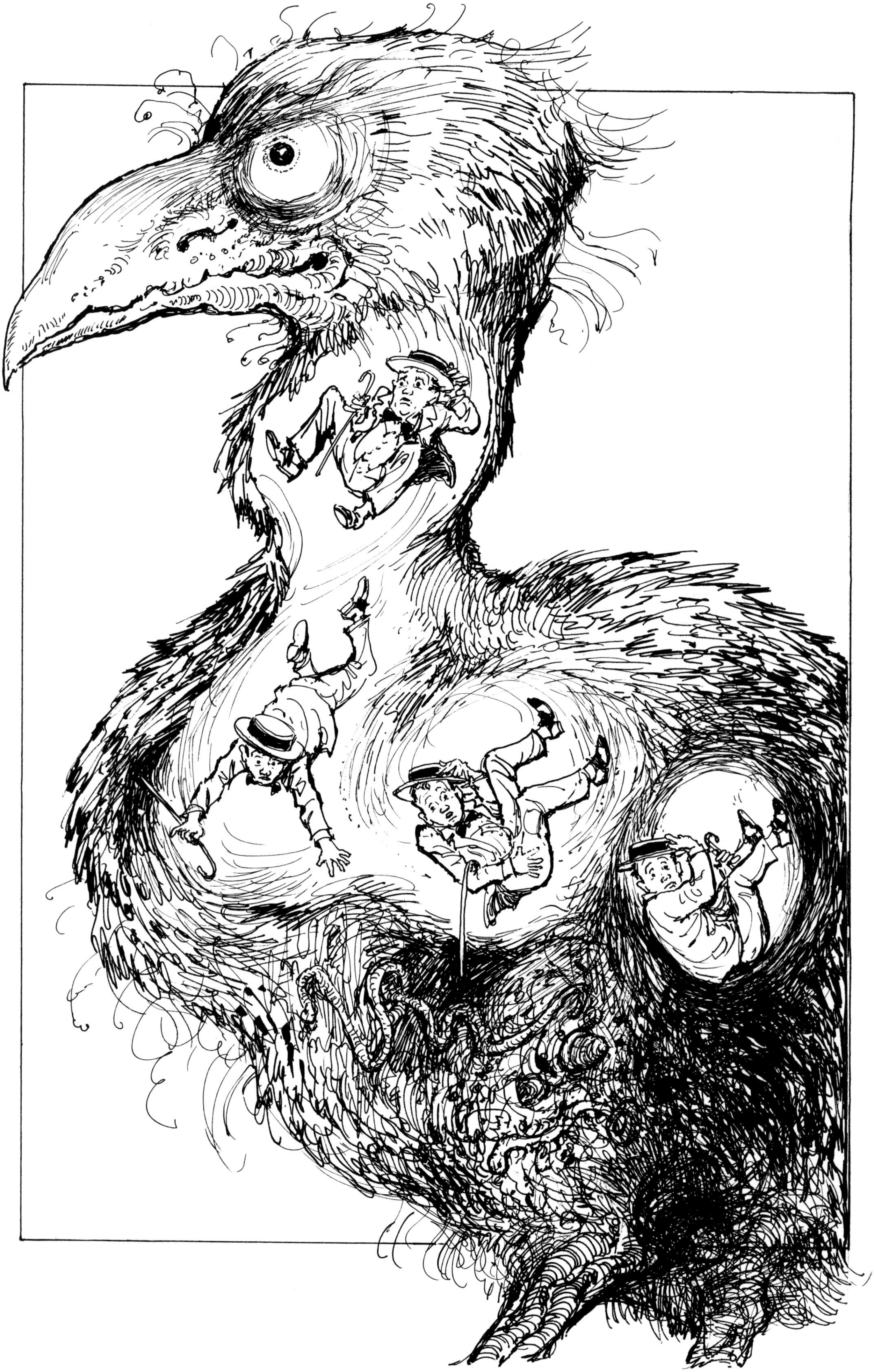

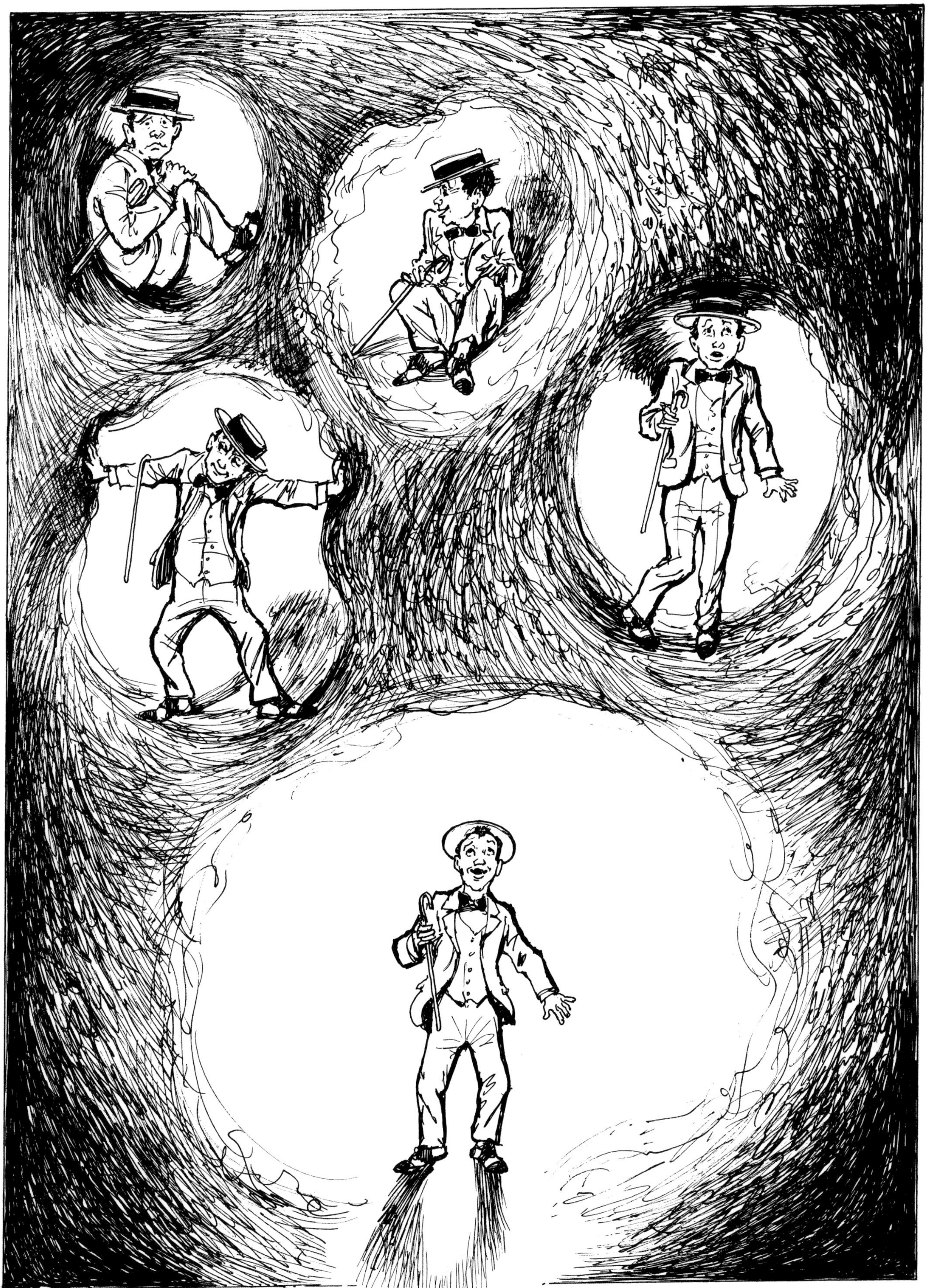

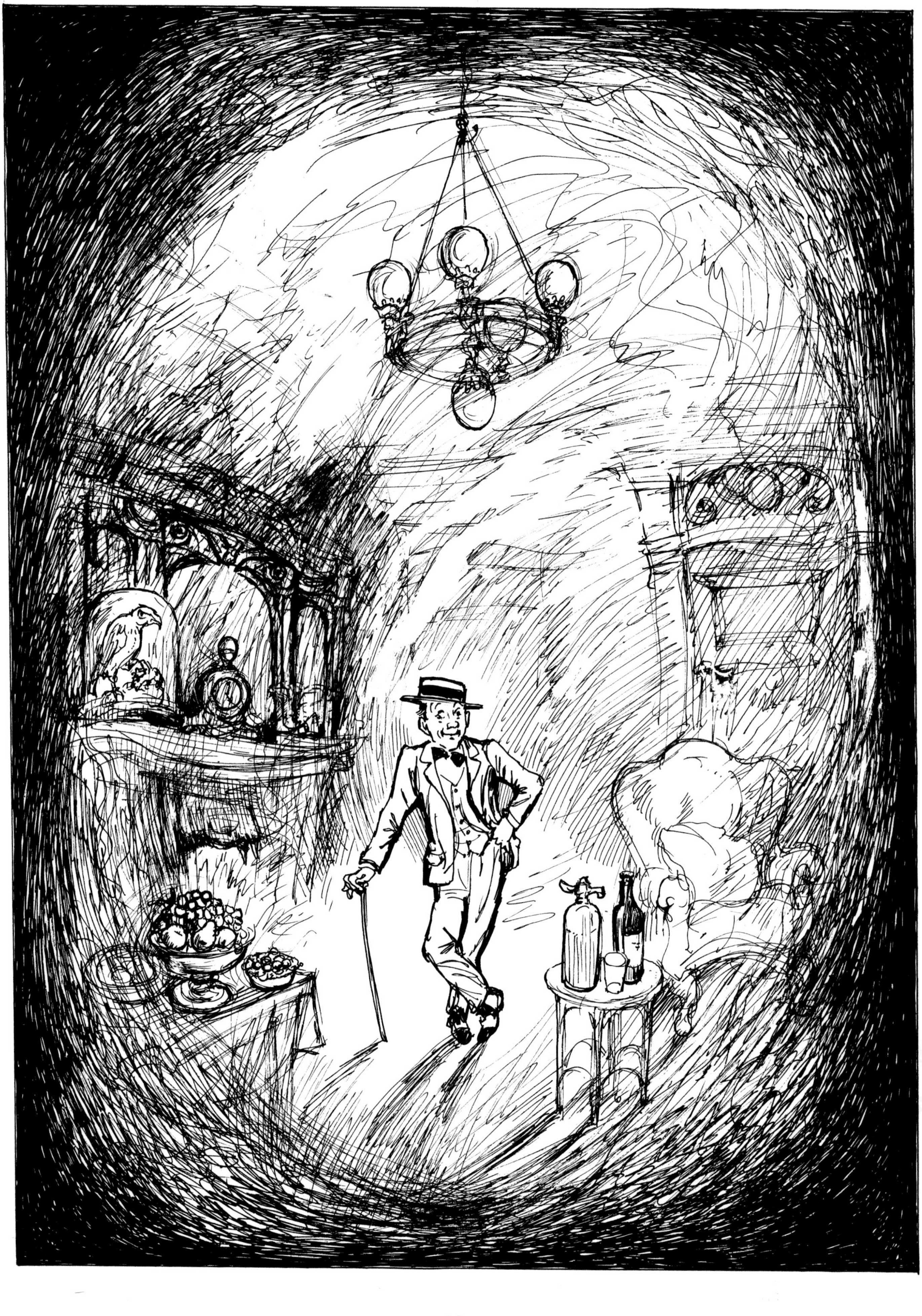

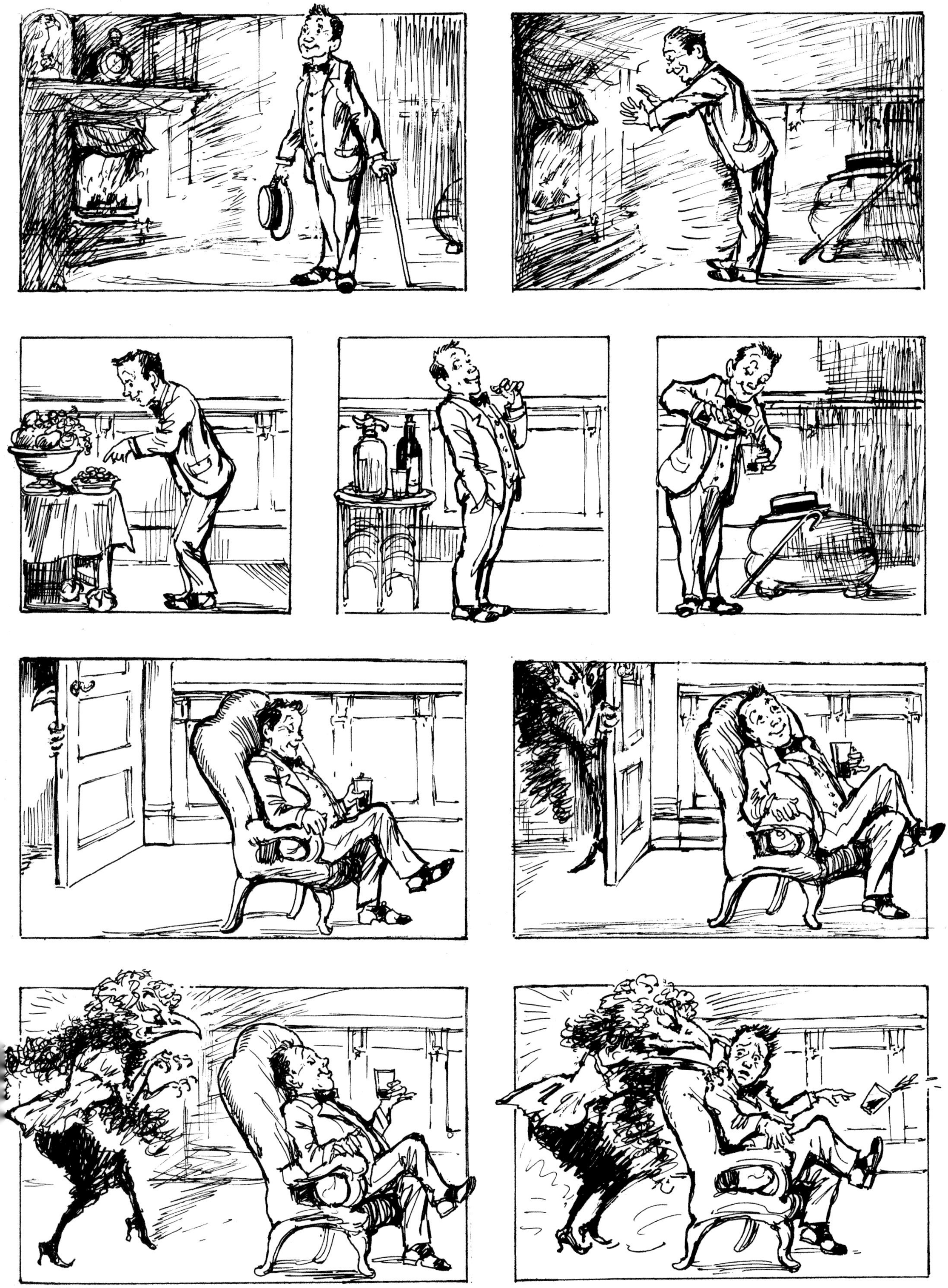

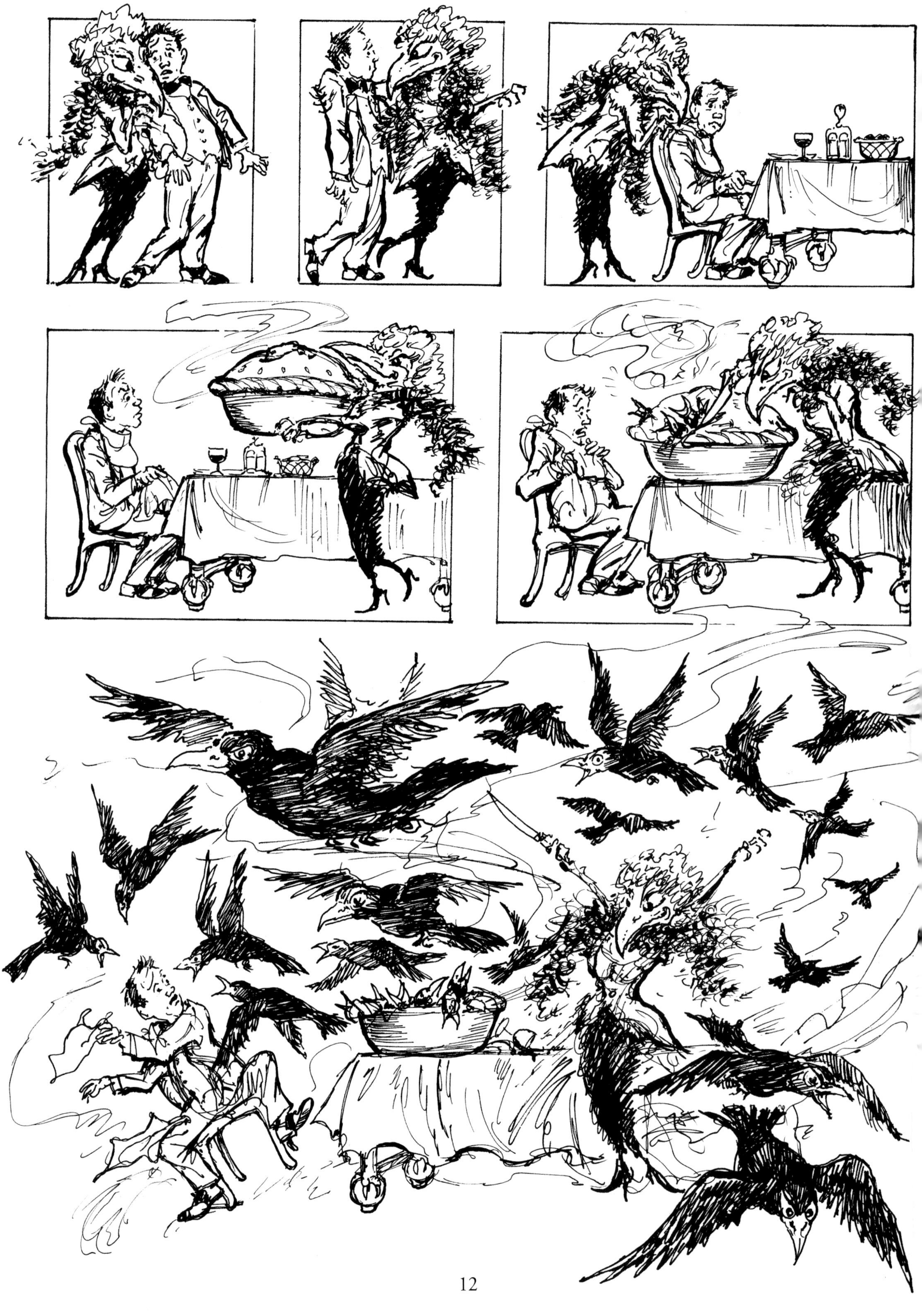

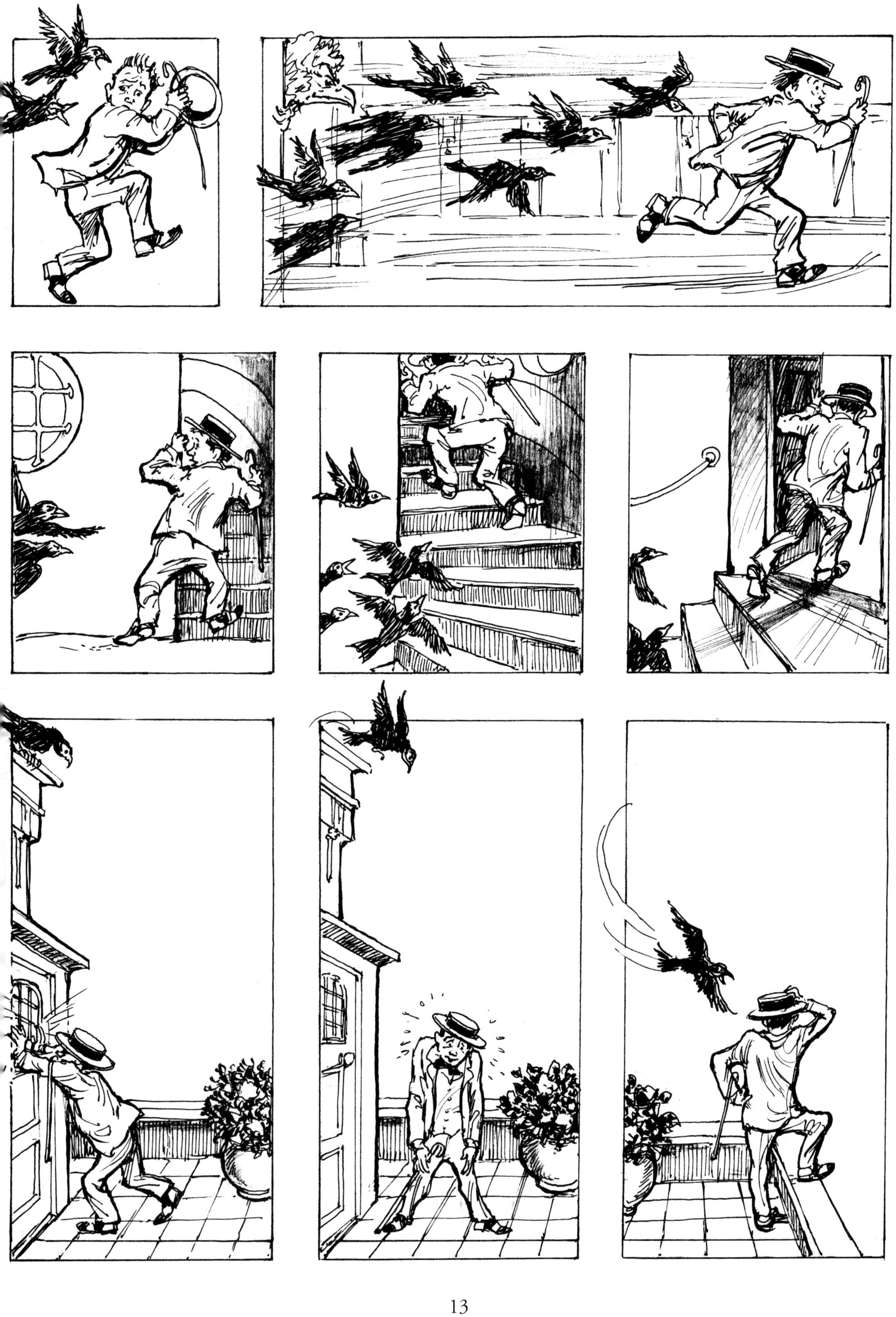

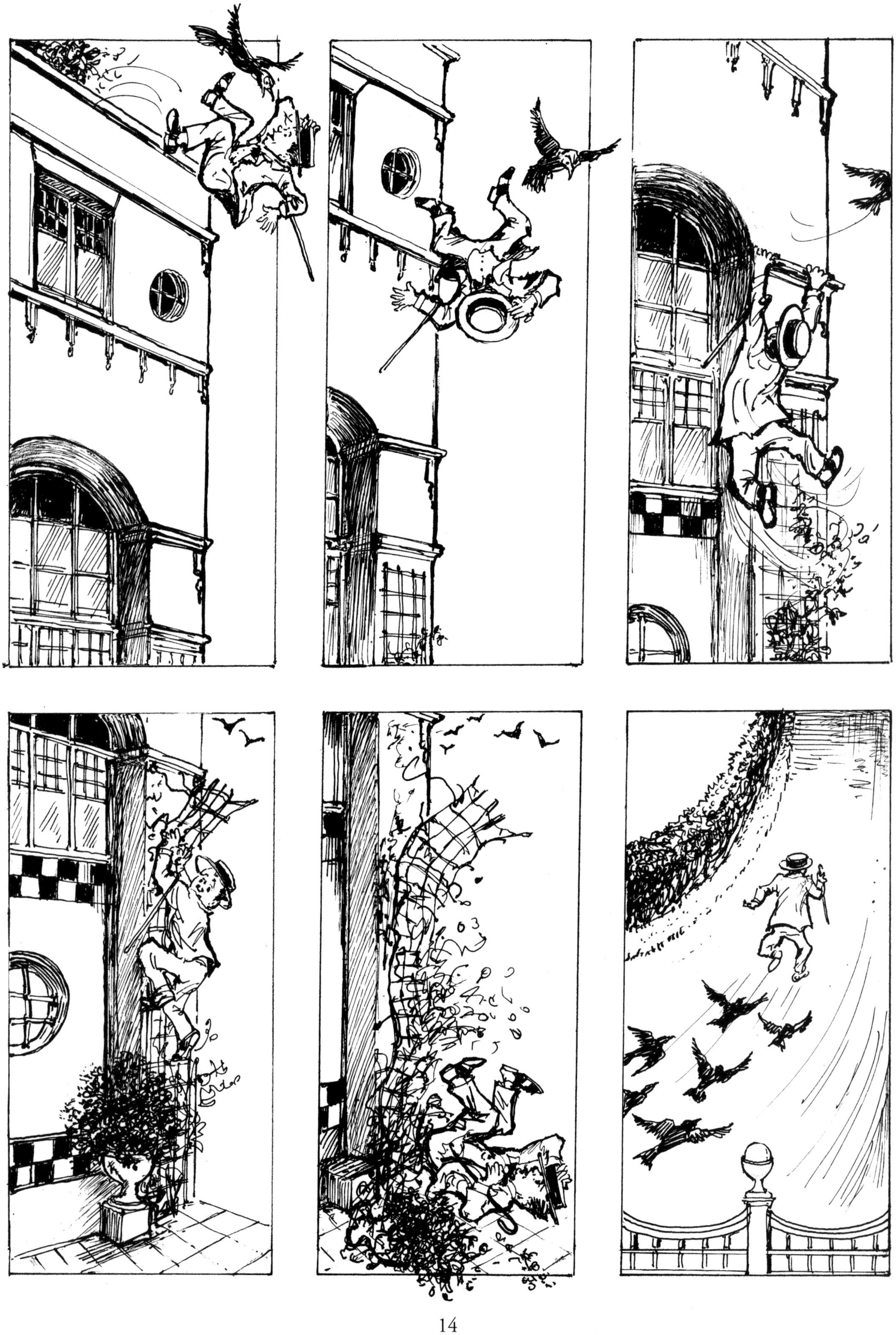

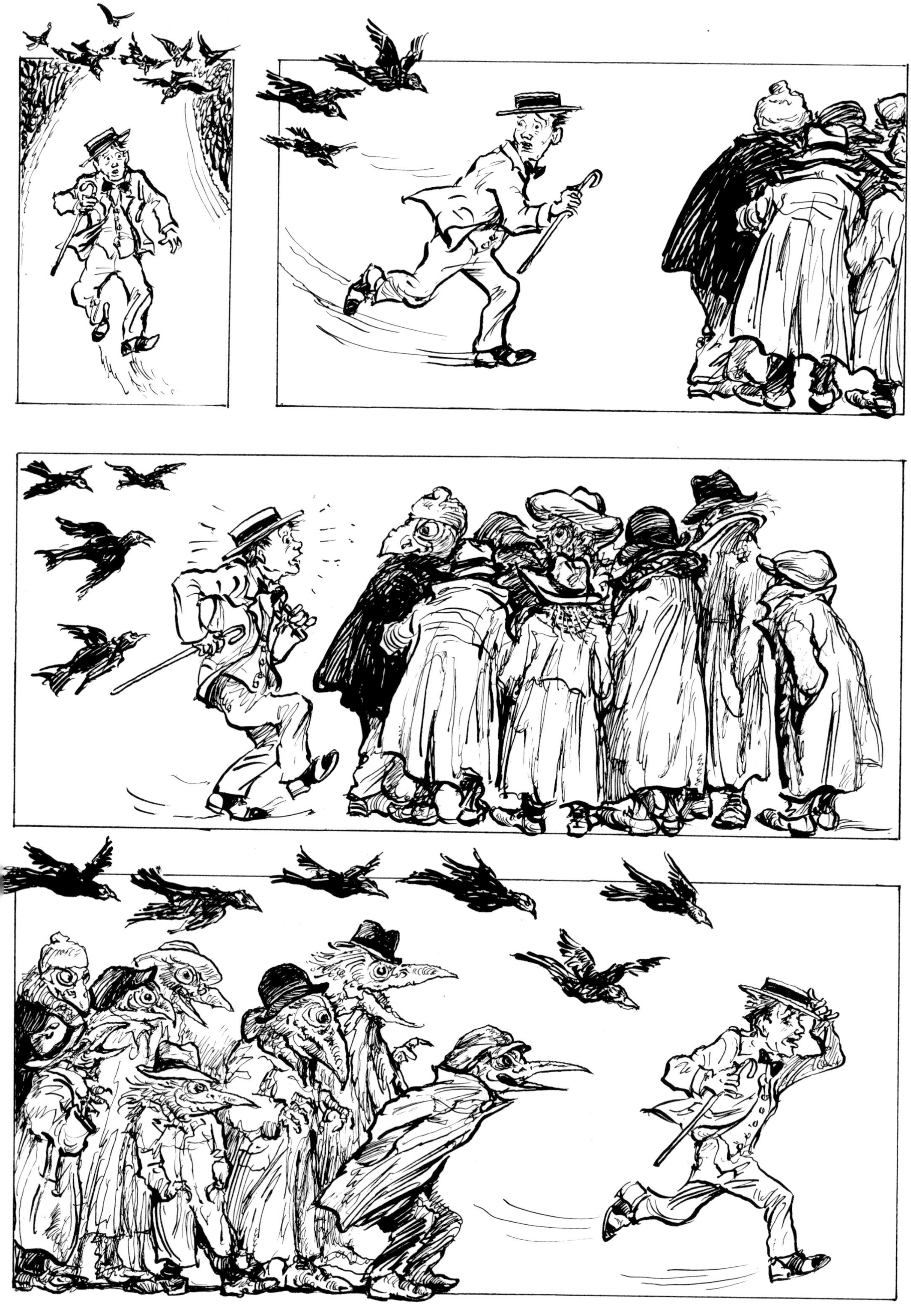

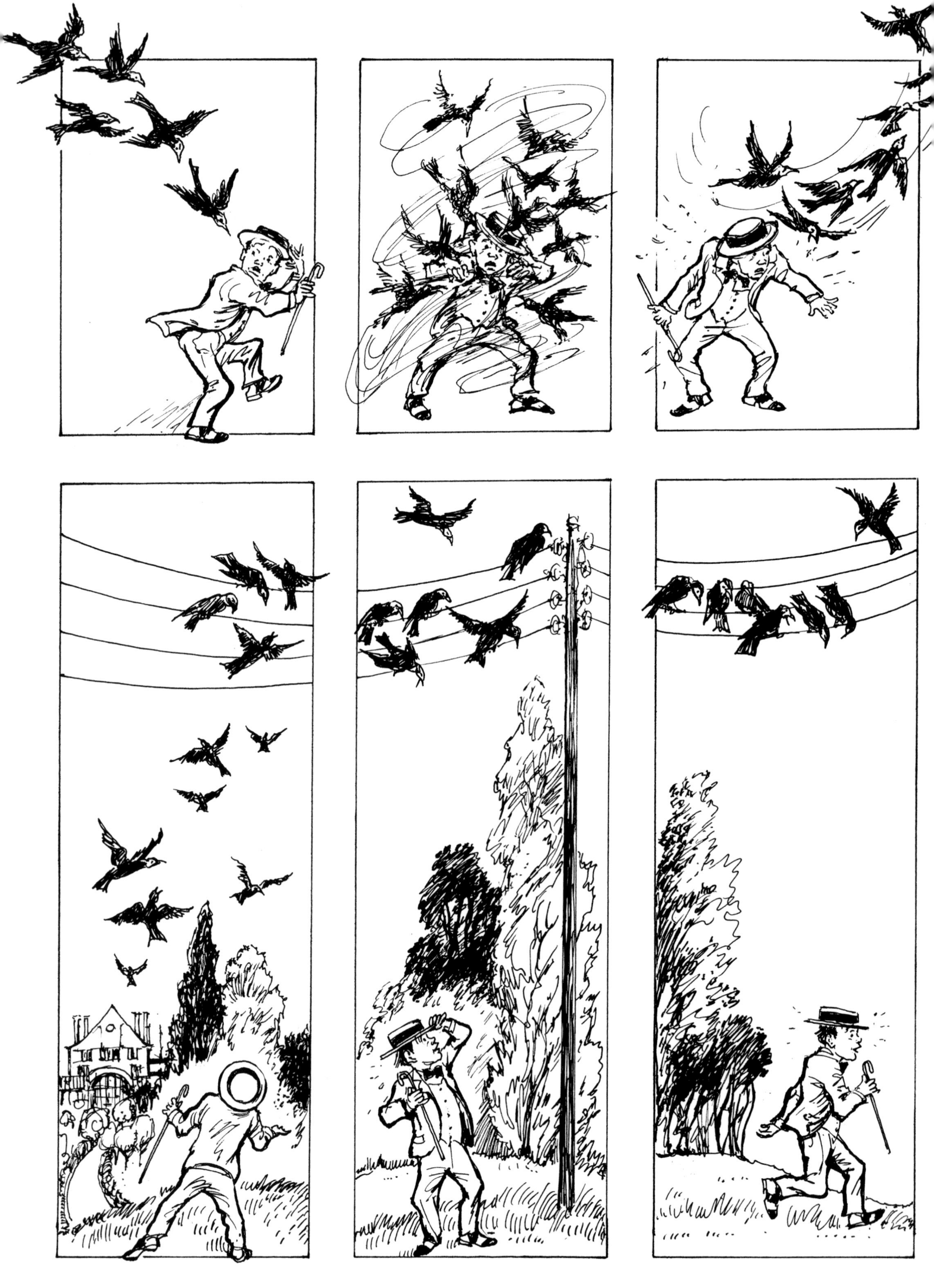

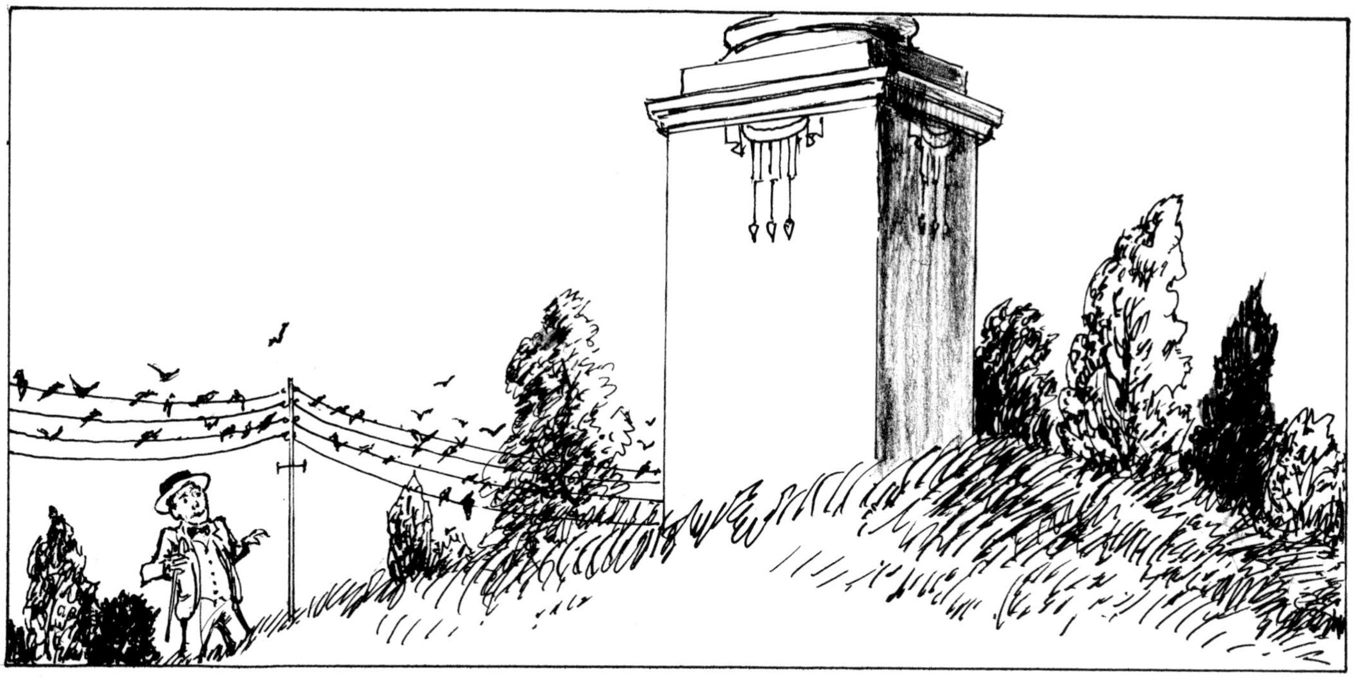

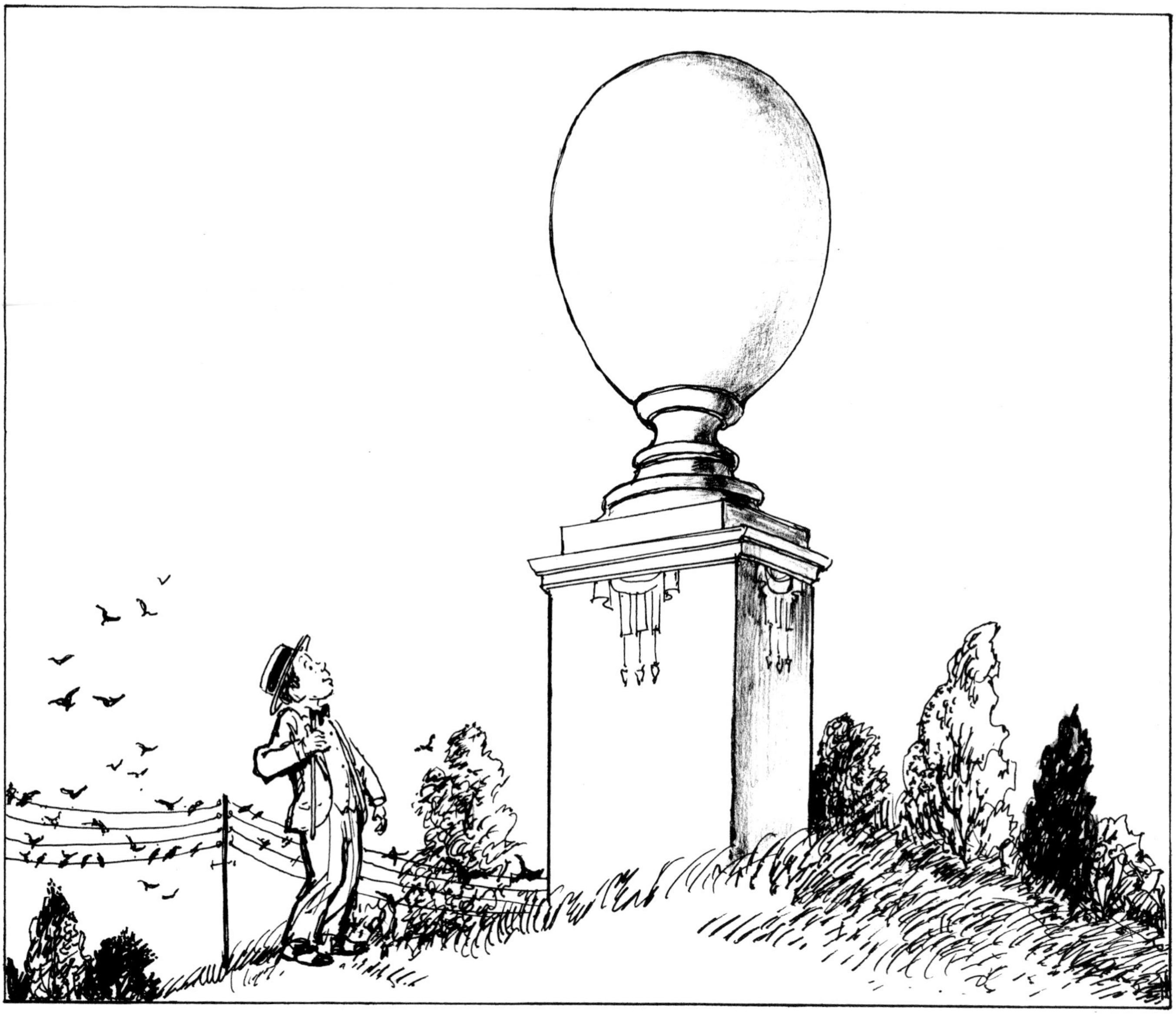

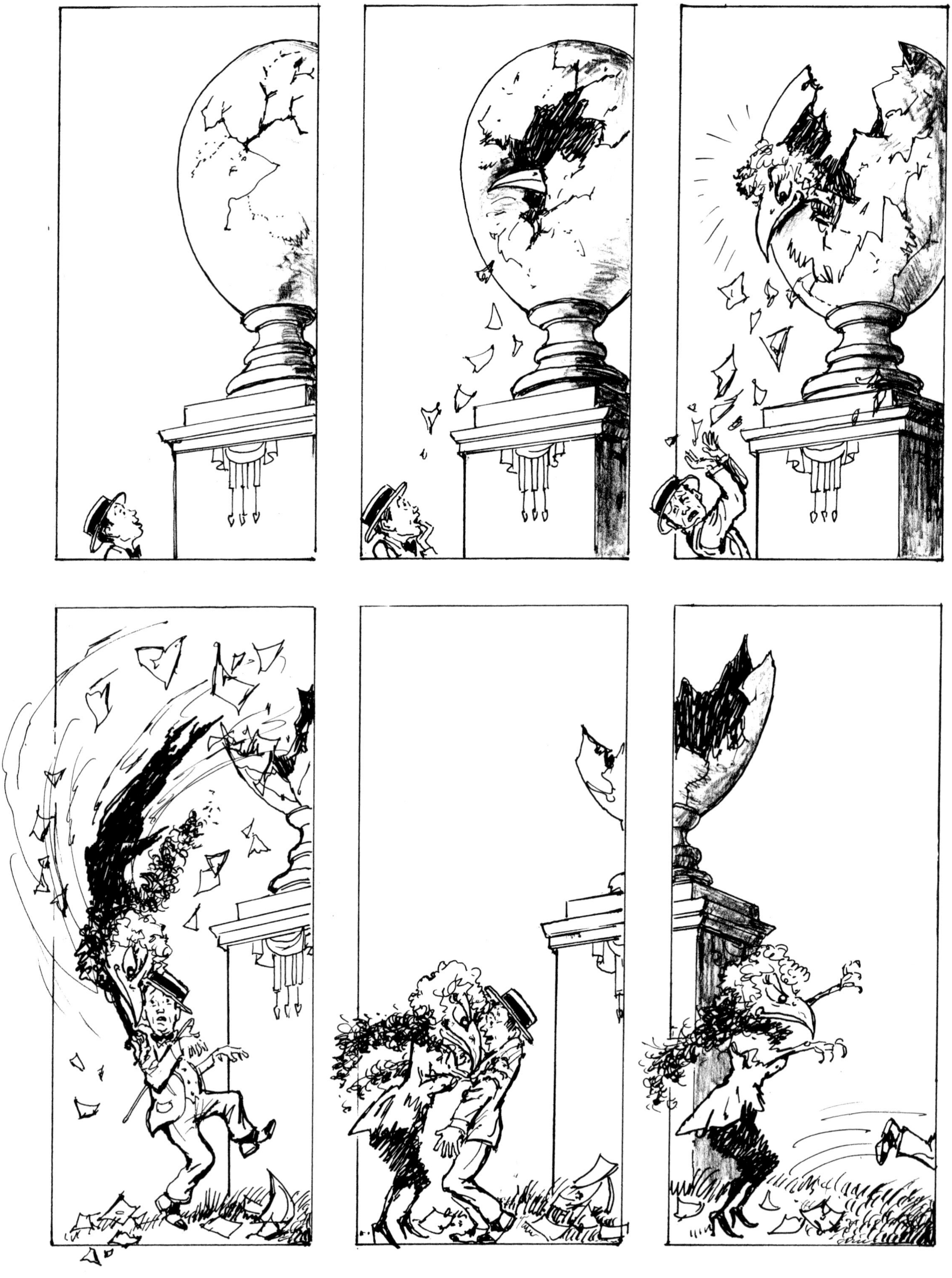

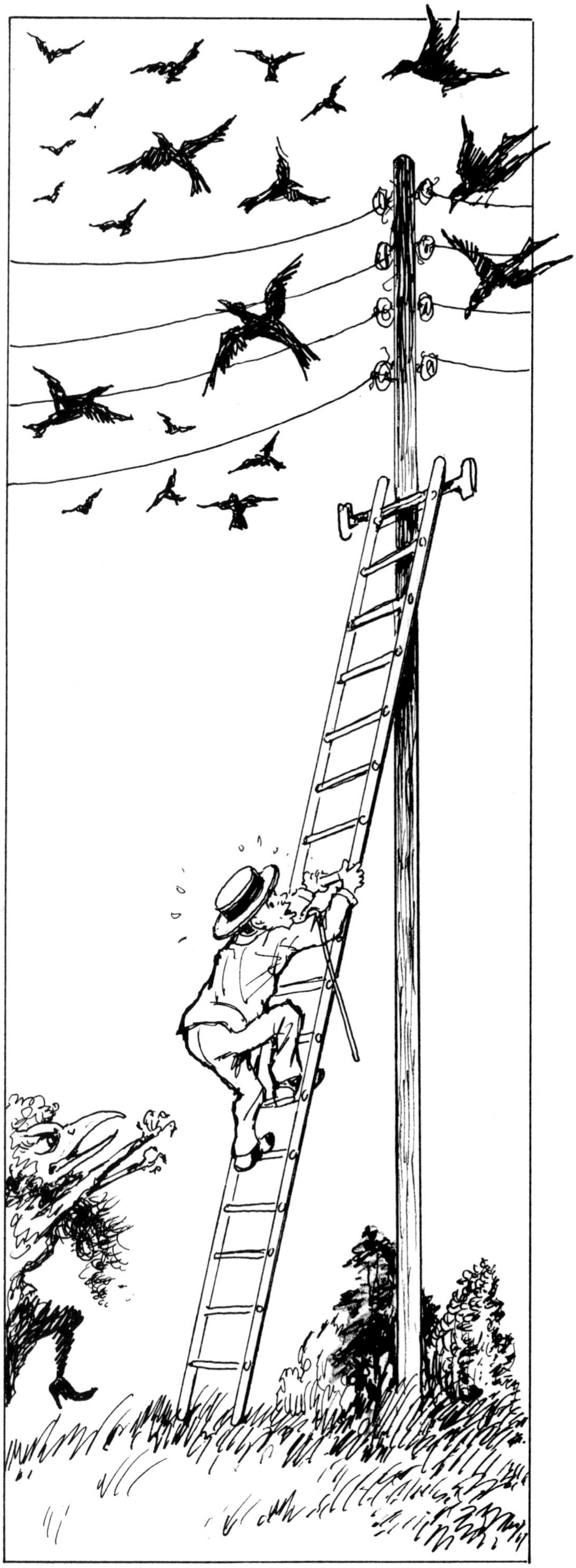

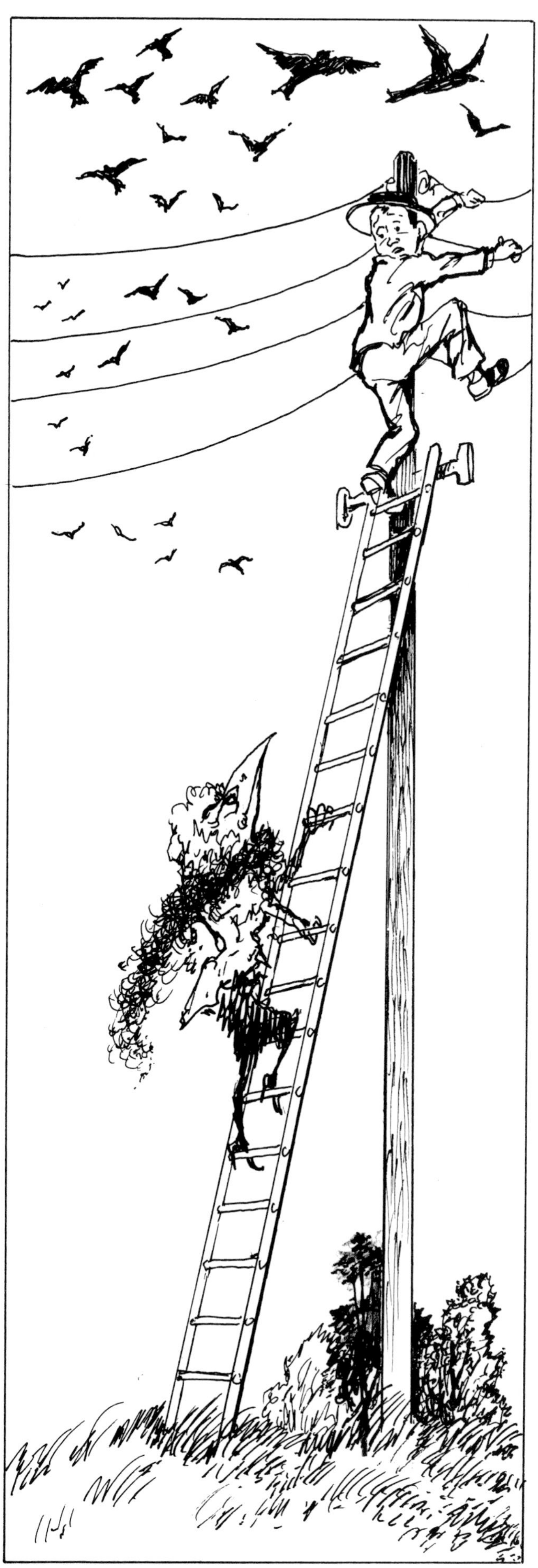

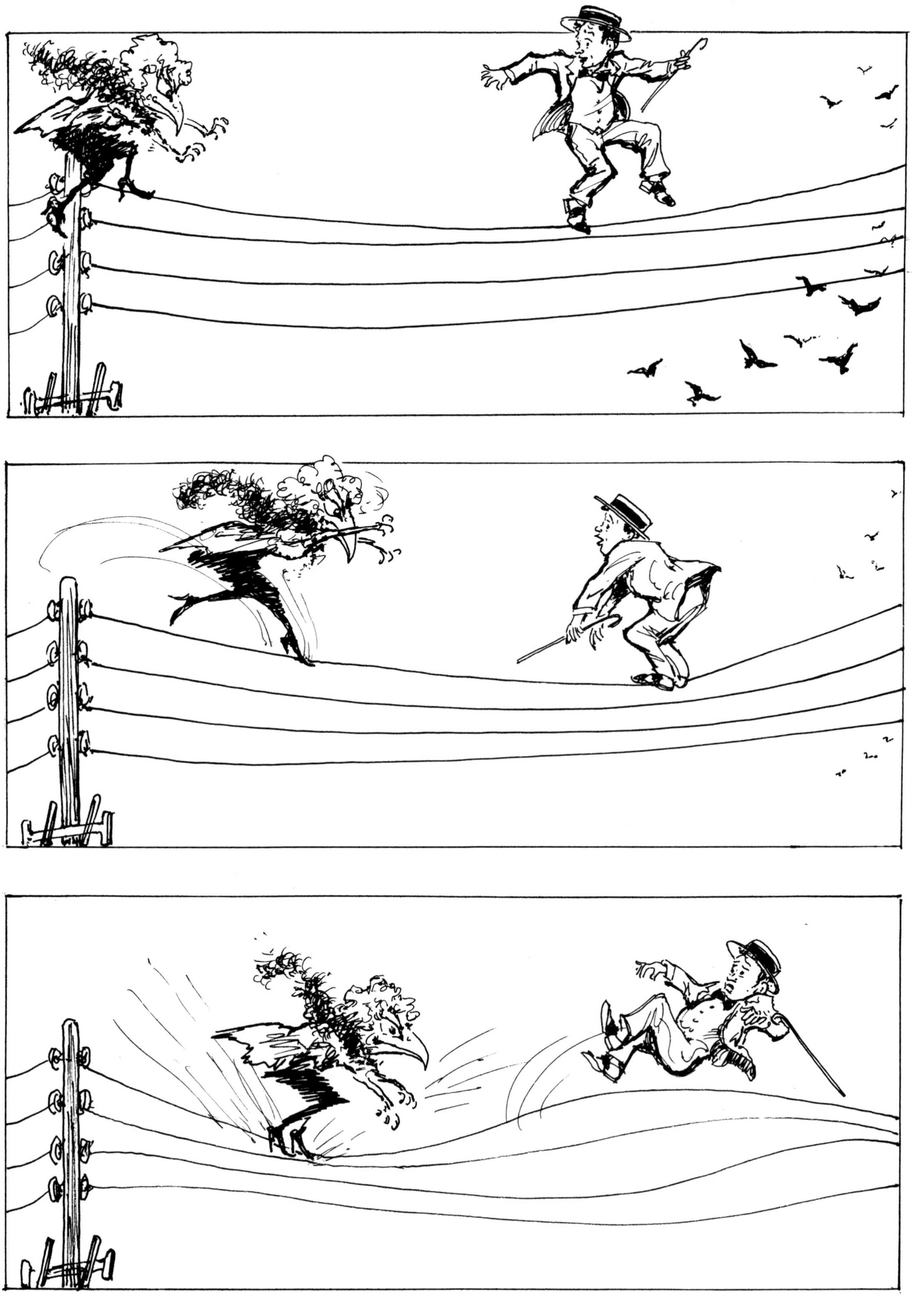

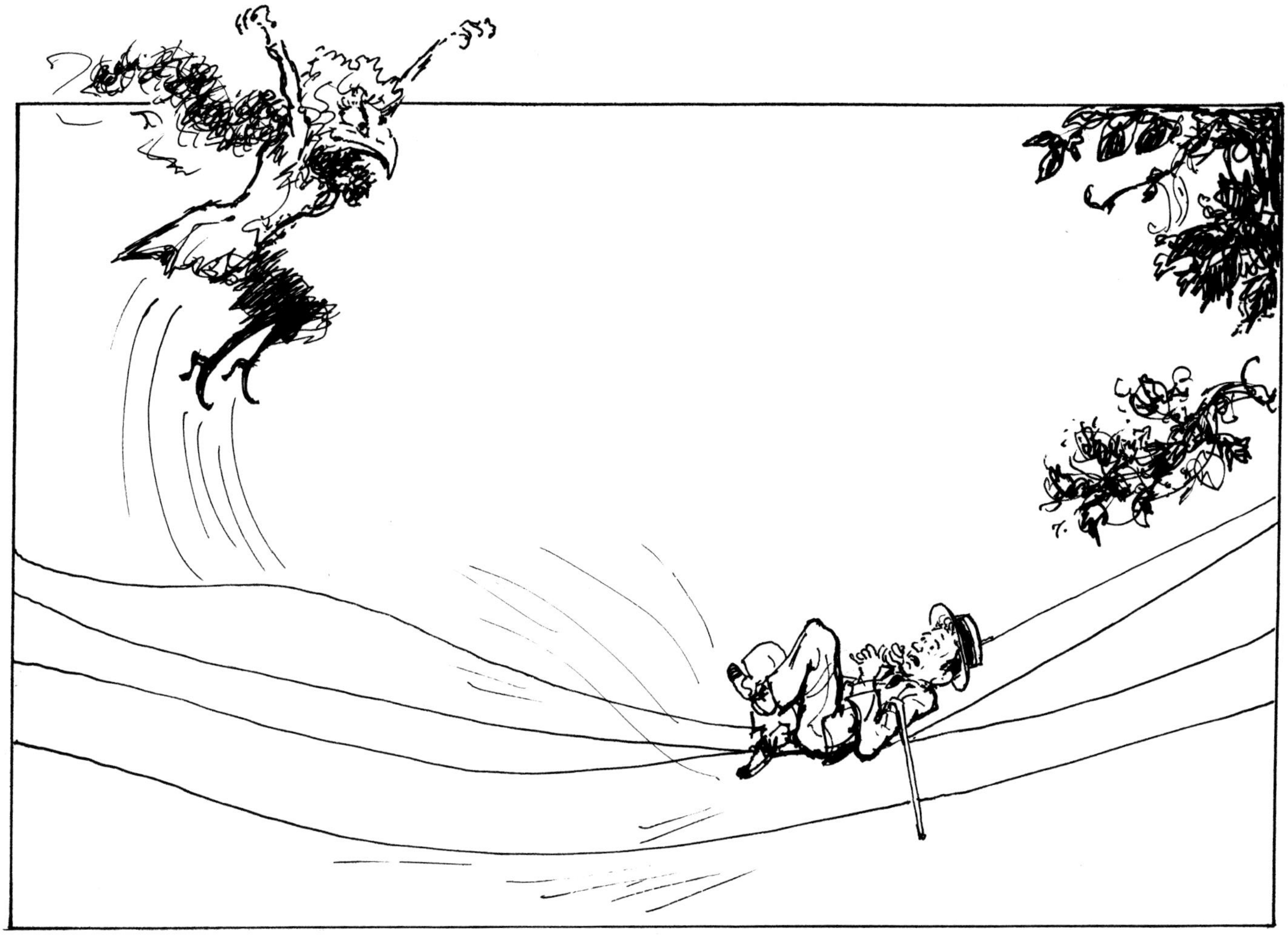

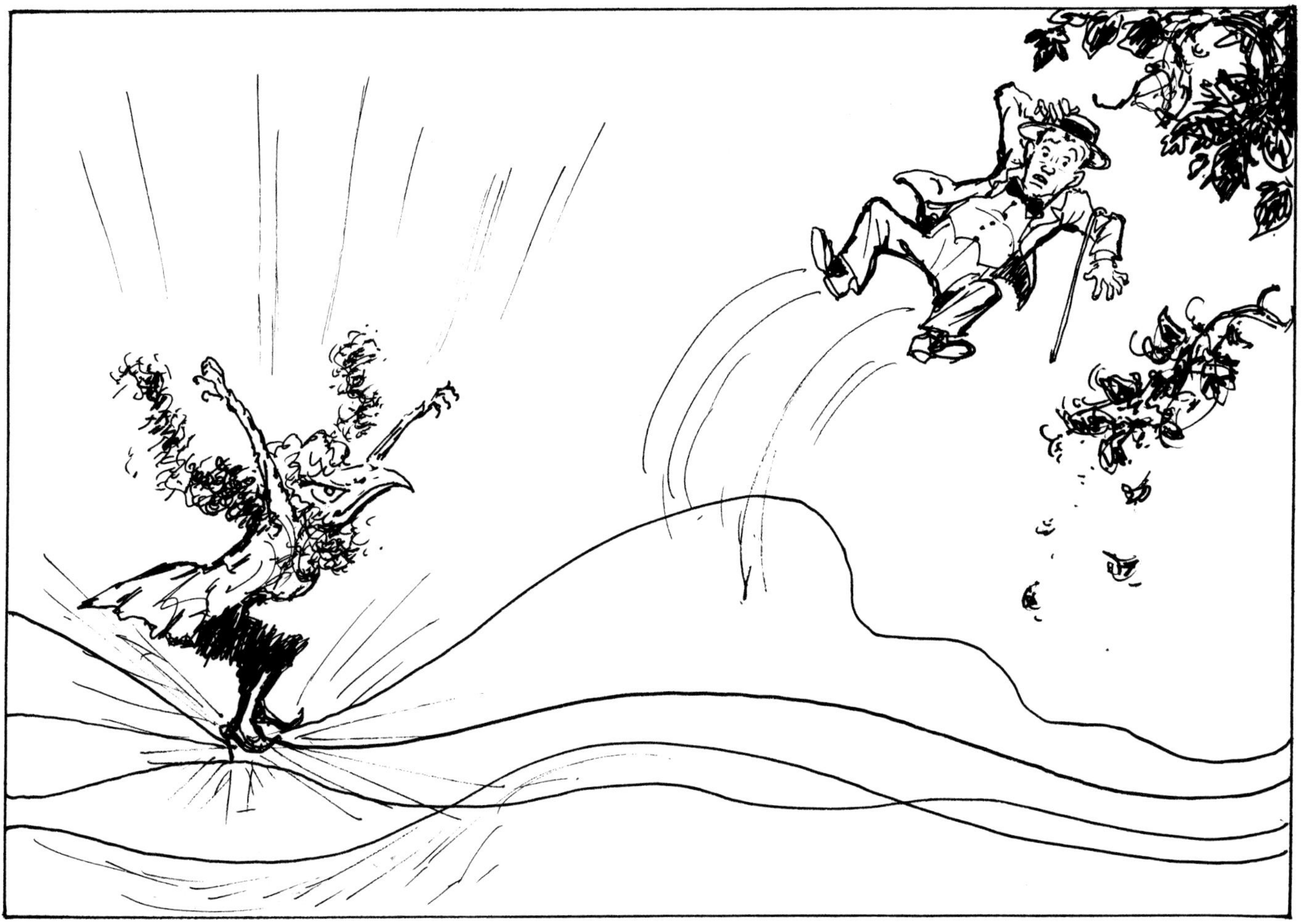

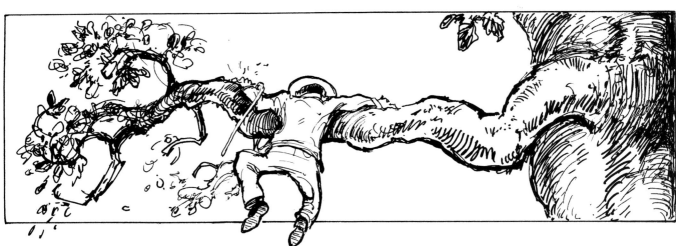

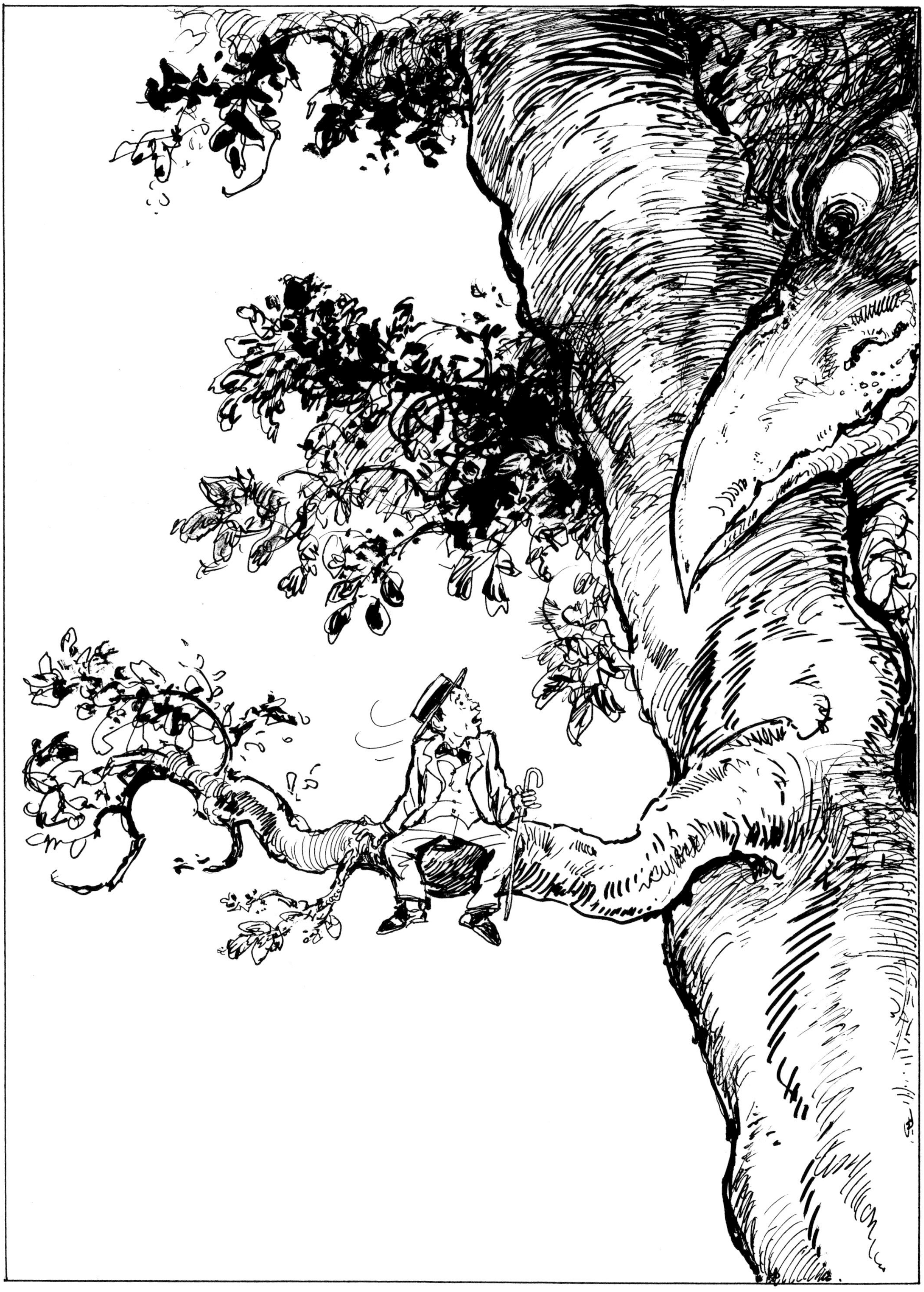

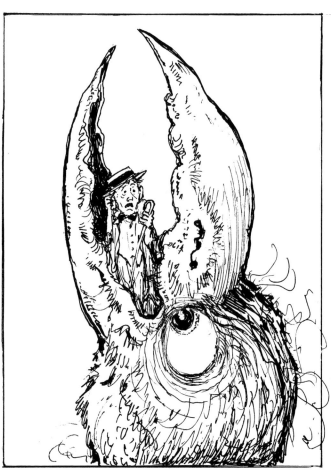

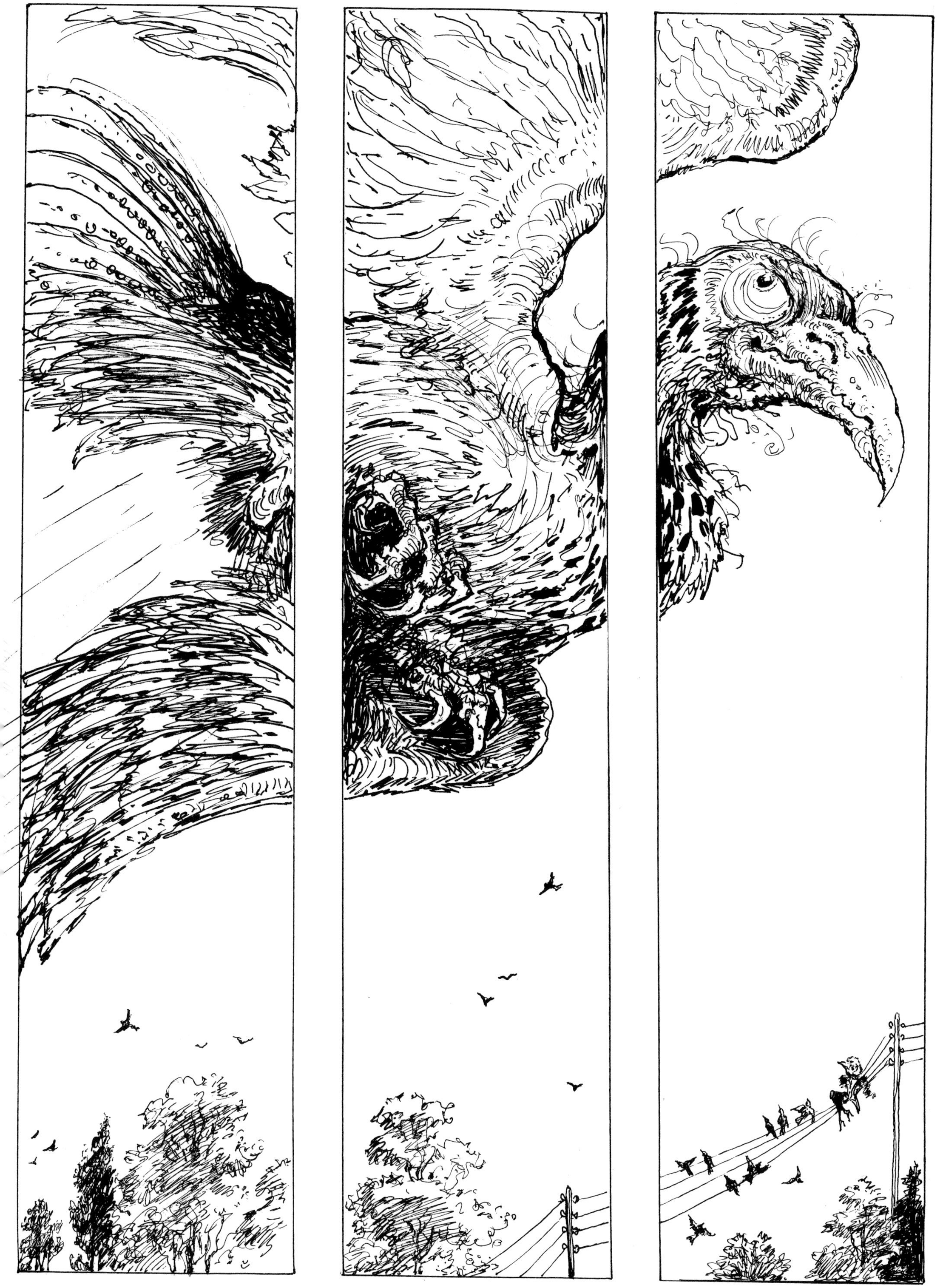